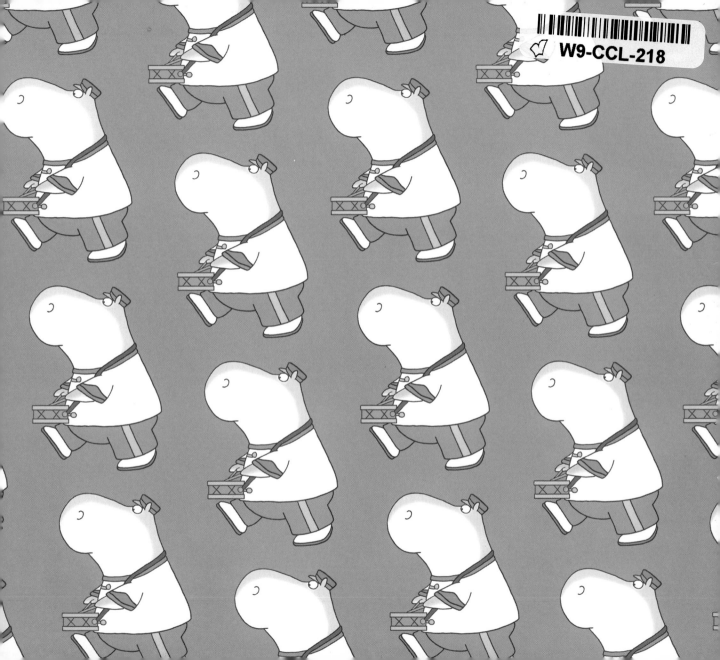

CHRISTMAS PARADE

CHRISTMAS PARADE

by Sandra Boynton

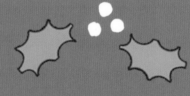

To the amazing Sarah Getz

LITTLE SIMON An imprint of Simon and Schuster Children's Publishing Division 1230 Avenue of the Americas, New York, New York 10020
Copyright © 2011, 2012 by Sandra Boynton. All rights reserved, including the right of reproduction in whole or in part in any form.
LITTLE SIMON is a registered trademark of Simon & Schuster, Inc. and associated colophon is a trademark of Simon & Schuster, Inc.
Cataloging-in-Publication Data is available for this book from the Library of Congress.
Manufactured in the USA 0912 LAK   First Edition 2 4 6 8 10 9 7 5 3 1   ISBN 978-1-4424-6813-9

BOOM biddy
BOOM BO
Biddy BOOM
biddy BOOM

4

BOOM biddy OM BOOM! biddy BOOM BOOM BOOM!

What's that noise filling the room?

I think that's the sound of the

CHRISTMAS PARADE!

Run to
the window!
Pull up
the shade!

YES!

First comes the elephant
marching along
with a

BOOM—biddy
BOOM—biddy

steady and strong.

And next come the chickens

with silver bassoons...

...followed by piggies
with Christmas balloons.

JOY! JOY! JOY!

Oh look! Drumming hippos,

with a **RAT-A-TAT-TAT.**

And even MORE hippos.

And one
drummer cat.

THE CHRISTMAS PARADE!

With holly confetti!
The Christmas Parade!
Here comes more!

Are you ready?

One
Santa
Claus
rhino!

Two cow saxophones!

Three piccolo mice!

And four ducks with trombones!

And then, last of all,
comes the TINIEST BIRD
with the

LOUDEST

tuba
you ever
have heard.

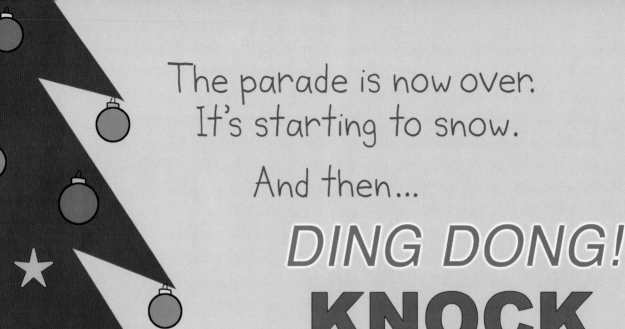

The parade is now over.
It's starting to snow.

And then...

DING DONG!

**KNOCK
KNOCK.**

Is it someone
we know?

Go to the door.

Open it wide.

Look who it is
standing outside!

29

We thank you for watch-ing. Our time here is through

The End

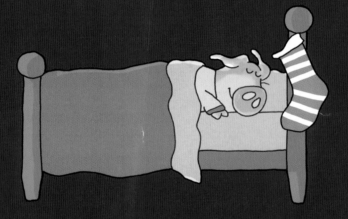

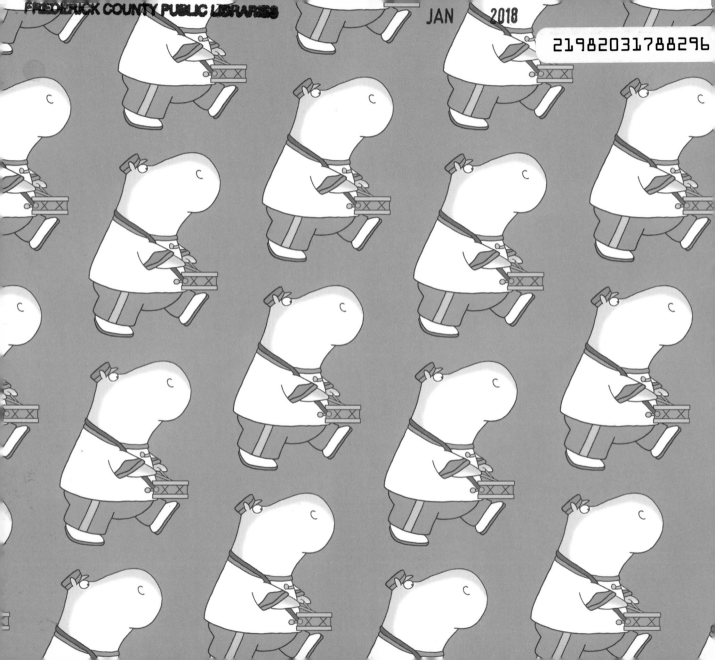